Miss Lucy

Slave and Civil War Nurse

A novel
based on a true story

Judith C. Owens-Lalude

Miss Lucy: Slave and Civil War Nurse

AnikePress
Worldwide Publisher
Henderson, Nevada, USA

Revised 2022, © Copyright 2013

Orders: *AnikePress*.com

ISBN   978-0-9848203-3-7
LCCN   2013915589

Miss Lucy: Slave and Civil War Nurse
Acknowledgements
Supportive institutions
Suggested reading
Discussion questions

Book cover, interior designs, and illustrations
by Judith C. Owens-Lalude

Lucy Higgs Nichols photograph courtesy of New Albany
Floyd County Public Library, New Albany, Indiana

To contact the author or receive information about book
signings and related programs contact the author at:
jcamille@AnikePress.com
jclalude@gmail.com

AnikePress
Worldwide Publisher
Henderson, Nevada

This book is written in honor of Lucy Higgs Nichols as well as the brave black men who volunteered or were recruited to serve in the Union Army (Colored Army). They fought for the freedom of black men, black women, and black children who, along with their ancestors, were enslaved by the European settlers. They and the sacrifices they made will never be forgotten.

Introduction

The following is a quote, taken in part from *A Historical Sketch of the 23rd Regiment, Indiana Volunteer Infantry, July 29th, 1861, to July 23rd, 1865,* by Shadrach K. Hooper, First Lieutenant and Adjutant, for the 1910 Report Indiana-Vicksburg Military Park Commission:

> There were few regiments in the War of the Rebellion whose service was more continuous, more constantly at the front, more frequently on the firing line, than that of the 23rd Regiment, Indiana Volunteer Infantry. During its four years of service, lacking but six days, it was continuously in the field, and it is questionable whether there was any regiment whose campaign was more extensive or covered so vast a territory as that of the 23rd, when it is considered that in leaving its rendezvous at New Albany, Indiana, for the field, it marched west and during the succeeding four years accomplished a complete circle of fully 3,000 miles, returning home from the east, and at no time retracing its steps except in detours from its great circular journey, and

that during its period of service it participated in practically all the campaigns of the armies of Generals Grant and Sherman.

The 23rd Regiment, raised in the southern part of the State of Indiana might be properly called a border regiment, its entire enlistment having come from the border counties of Floyd, Clark, Harrison, and Crawford, with the exception of a large portion of one company and a few members of the other companies who came from Washington County, and a score or more loyal Kentuckians.

Table of Contents

1

Never Sold

The night bell rang. It sounded an end to the workday. Not much light was left in the sky. Aaron and Angeline had decided to find me. I had asked them to tell me about where I had come from.

I was chasing a lamb around the yard when Aaron beckoned to me. I dropped the cornbread crumbs I was feeding to the whiner and rushed to meet him. He took hold of my hand. I followed him along the alley to where Angeline waited for us. She caught hold of my other hand. The three of us smiled as we ambled toward the river. It wasn't often we could sneak time together. But on this day, Master Marcus Higgs and the missus were in town completing their errands.

Whenever they were away, life around the quarters didn't have the usual chaos. Instead, there was a calm and slow quietness in the air. Only the croak of the frogs and neigh of the horses could be heard. We moved closer to the creek that dumped into the river. We didn't need the light of the sun to find the boulder. We knew our way and raced there. The babbling waves that washed over the creek's bottom would muffle our words if anyone tried to eavesdrop.

Aaron skipped ahead of me. He wanted to be the first seated at the stone table. I caught hold of his shirttail. "Tell me, 'bout myself," I said hurriedly. He kept moving as he glanced across the waters to spot unwanted visitors that might be moving too close to us. After Aaron positioned himself at the stone, Angeline and I huddled, one on each side of him. The three of us butted together. We stretched our limbs so our fingertips touched. The love and warmth rushed up my arms to the tip-top of my head. I pulled my limbs back and glanced at Aaron. He knew what I wanted to hear.

"Where do you want me to start tellin'?" he asked.

"Start where I started."

At first, Aaron said nothing, just seemed to study his hands. I sat back on my heels and seized the moment. Angeline was focused on our faces. Aaron cocked his head. As the moonlight polished his cheeks, he continued his thinking. Then he moved his lips.

Before he said anything, I asked, "Where we be livin' when I's born?"

With soft whispers, Aaron finally spoke.

"I'm sure we was somewhere in Halifax County, North Carolina. And pretty sure it be 1838. That be where we was when you come to us. It was Master Jacobs who owned us . . . and Ma too. At the time you was born, it be a warm and sunny day–not sure exactly which one. But everybody in the quarters knowed when you come to this world. Your yap was loud as a piglet's squeal. You could be heard across the fields and over the big hill. Ma said she felt glad to have you. We didn't know if you was gonna make it to this world or not. Ma wanted to name you Lucky, but said it wasn't a good name for you, so she called you Lucy. Said it sounded like music."

"What was Master Jacob's family like?"

"He wasn't no meaner or nicer than any of the other slave owners. He had his good days. And he could be ornery as a hungry bear on other days."

"And Ma?" I asked Aaron, like I always did.

The questions never changed and the answers were always the same.

"You never knowed her. Cain't tell you much about her neither, 'cept she be a good person. Angeline and me, we never spend much time with her. When she wasn't workin' around the farm, she was hired out. We couldn't see or talk to her when we wanted to. Angeline and me . . . we hardly knowed each other. Most every day, Angeline was running errands for Master Jacob's missus. I be runnin' them for him. He be a well-to-do farmer with a boy named Reuben.

"Master Reuben married a woman named Eliza. Their daughter was Wineford Amanda. It wasn't no time 'fore he divorced the missus and married a lady named Miss Elizabeth. She be his cousin. By then you was nearly seeing your second spring, makin' you near to a year old. I knowed that because them tiny lavender flowers with sun-yellow centers was showin' themselves along the creek, just like they did the day you was born.

"After Master Reuben's wedding to Miss Elizabeth, we was given to him. You, me, and Angeline. After some time, they had three children: Marcus, Wyly, and Prudence. The missus, she died trying to give birth to her number four. It died, too. Master Reuben buried them. Then he got himself married to a third wife, but she died, and it wasn't long after that, he died.

"Master Reuben's boy, Marcus Higgs . . . he got us, the Higgs land, and the other slaves. By this time you were 'bout eight, maybe nine years. You done lived in different states: North Carolina, Tennessee, Mississippi. Could have been more. But for sure, you was never sold."

Angeline scooted around the boulder, nearer to me. Even though it was dark, I could see her looking into my eyes. I knew they were moonlit, because I could see moonbeams in hers.

She told me, looking in my eyes, "In 1844, Miss Wineford Amanda Higgs inherited the three of us. She was a young gal. The two of you be about the same age. Like Aaron told you before, when her ma and pa died, the three of us belong to her. Nobody else was around to take charge. Two years later Little Miss Wineford Amanda died. The three of us was put in the care of a man named Samuel G. Wheeless. He be a neighbor. Somewhere along the way, he decided he wanted to own us. You, me and Aaron. We ended up in Tennessee where Massa Wheeless hired some man he call G. W. Hill. Massa Hill loaded us into a wagon and hauled us from Bolivar, Tennessee, to Coffeeville, Mississippi. Took near eight days and some eighty miles is what I hear them say. I be so troubled, I couldn't tell one day from the next. They all come together making one troubling time for me."

I anchored my elbows on my knees and rested my chin on the heels of my palms. My fingers held onto my cheeks. I looked at my brother and then my sister. I had taken in every word they had said.

Lucy twilled her fingers, and then looked up at her siblings, "I remember how the Higgs family and Master Wheeless argued. They fought about who we belong to. Next thing I know, I was standing in front of a judge."

Angeline and Aaron glanced at me. Aaron said, "It was around 1848 when we walked into the courtroom. Hot bodies be bunched together. The men were shoving, and pushing, and smoking cigars and pipes. They be standing around talking ugly and spitting, too, when there was no spittoon that I could see. Guess them blobs be landing on da floor. Took some days before they decide who owned us. We were eventually returned to the Higgs children."

Angeline and I study Aaron's face when he paused to say, "I gasped when the Mississippi judge slammed his wooden knocker down on the block."

Angeline straightened herself like she did earlier and then leaned once again on the rock. She told us, "The judge told Master Wheeless he had to give us back to the Higgs children. Three of them were still alive at that time: Master Marcus, Master Wyly, and Missus Prudence."

Aaron raised his head. He said, "When all that happened, them wildflowers was up again. They was beamin' wid dem pretty colors, same as the day you was born. Things didn't get no better. Whenever somethin' happen wid one of dem, Higgs, they give us to another Higgs."

I closed my eyes and shifted my weight to sort my thoughts. When I opened them again, I looked from Aaron to Angeline and then lowered my eyelids once more. The tears that slipped from beneath them dampened my cheeks.

"I remember being hired out. I knew I was too young to be. Them white folks was as hateful as them Higgs. Those the times I don't want to talk about. The others, I done made myself forget." My voice cracked as I smudged my tears with the backside of my fingers.

Angeline held my shoulder and folded her other arm around me. She put her lips close to my ear and told me with her warm breath, "Don't you cry, gal. Your day be comin' soon. You done growed up to be a fine gal. One day you gonna be a fine lady, like you always dream of. I been prayin' it for you. And it gonna be so. That's what Ma say we should do when we wants things to be gittin' better. 'Just pray', she say to us."

2

Changing Owners

It never mattered which Higgs owned me. The treatment was brutal, not better than a fettered farm animal–never enough sleep or food or a decent place to sleep. Our cabin was stifling in the summer and unbearably cold in the winter. Everything came through the roof: leaves, rain, sunshine, snow, and bugs that bite, leaving behind bumps, welts, and sometimes weeping blisters. Nonetheless, I grew to womanhood same as most slave gals did.

A fella named Calvin came around the farm and soon took a fancy to me. It seemed he showed up whenever I was in the yard bent over the washtub. At first, I was too burdened with work to notice his swooning. Then one day, he came up in the yard where I was.

"How ya be, Miss Lucy?" he'd say when he could get close enough to me for his words to be private. Then he would be off.

Another day, when I was filling the washtub, I noticed him coming up the carriage lane. He was walking loose-legged with a wide stride and frantically waving his arms. I set the bucket down. I gripped at my chest. My heart pounded something awful. I was certain Calvin was fetching bad news and wanted me to deliver it to Master Marcus or maybe the missus.

"What be troublin' you, Calvin? You packin' sour news?" My words rushed at him.

Bent over, Calvin held onto his knees, unable to speak. His back rose, collapsed, and then rose again. Out of breath, he shook his head back and forth like a stallion separated from his mare. My shaky hands ladled up cool well water.

"Best you have yourself some of this here."

Calvin clasped his hands around mine and sipped from the bowl of the ladle.

"Lucy, I been wantin' to talk to ya for some time now."

"Ain't been nowhere. Ain't goin' nowhere. Be right here. Seemin' like 'til I die."

"Can we talk after the night bell? I got things I be wantin' to say to ya."

"Don't see why not. You done scared me so, I be thinkin' the devil's comin' after me."

"Don't mean ya no harm. Just be wantin' to talk."

I glanced around to be sure no eyes were

watching us. Someone crossed Missus's bedroom window. I lowered the bucket, still full of water, back down into the well. I quickly said with my head almost in the well as far as the bucket, "Just 'fore I come out of the big house, Master Marcus was tellin' Missus, when they done eatin', they gonna visit the neighbor not far from here. He say Mr. Edwards got himself a new horse and be wantin' to show it off."

Calvin took a step back. "When they gone, you come down to the river. I be at the big tulip tree."

Not raising my head, I told him, "I be there. Go on now 'fore trouble be findin' me . . . and you. And there won't be no talkin' . . . . not 'tween us." To not be suspected of *going-ons,* I didn't budge until Calvin had moved away. When I began to feel dizzy I brought my head up.

Calvin was walking away with a sureness, almost like a white man's. I stared at him until I couldn't see his back. Even though the mid-evening air was cool, I was sweating, where I didn't usually sweat. My blood was bubbling up inside me. I thought about the tulip tree with its tiny, yellow-green bumps waiting to burst open with bowls full of orange-colored glow and a sweet-as-honey fragrance that scented the air. When I was done watching and thinking, I continued with the laundry. Before I finished it, Missus called me from an upstairs window.

"I's coming, Missus."

I left the unfinished laundry sitting in the yard and hurried up to the bedroom.

"I'll be needing a bath. Mr. Higgs and I are going out soon. Don't make it too hot. Hurry, gal."

I put a stewing pot on the fire to heat some water. Then I fetched several buckets of well water up the back stairs and filled the copper bathtub. I added the boiling water to the bathwater. When it was warm enough, I dripped lavender oil on the surface of it. That's what the

Missus told me I should do. When she detected the floral aroma, she slid down into the tub. After I washed her back, she took time to spoil her pale skin. When wrinkled and shriveled like a long turkey's neck, she stepped out of the tub. I towel-dried her as she grumbled about whatever was on her mind that day.

Missus step into a pair of drawers, and I tied them on her at the waist. Then I helped her into a chemise. Afterward, I laced her up in a corset. As I pulled on the strings, I thought about the times she had slapped me with her mean hand. I tugged harder. I wanted desperately to choke her 'til she was next to death's door. Instead, I knotted the strings.

Missus tiptoed over to the crinoline cage collapsed on the floor. Trying to be cute, she pointed her big toe at the mid-ring. She bobbled when she stepped into the center of it. I steadied her and then lifted the hoop skirt up and fixed it at her waist.

From the bed, I gathered up a mound of sky-blue skirting. I held it above Missus' head. When I let go, it dropped onto her up-reaching arms and down over her tilted head. Layers of ruffles waffled over the hoop skirt. I secured the blue skirt and then buttoned the fussy pearls that tracked up the back of the matching bodice. The v-shape neckline fanned shoulder-to-shoulder. It exposed a decent amount of her back and small bosom.

My hands hesitated. My eyes were drawn to the windowpanes. The sun was dropping from the evening sky. It tinted the window panes with a glowing rose-colored hue and brushed the underbelly of the clouds with pinks and yellows. I pondered if Calvin was leaning against the tulip tree, seeing the same wonderment.

"What's got you staring out that window, gal?"

"Don't know, Missus. Guess I be studyin'

the sunset just 'yond them trees. It be lookin' mighty pretty."

"It does. But I think it would be best if you kept your mind on what you need to be doing for me, and let the Lord manage the sunset. Hurry, gal! Get this mess cleaned up. Be sure to take care of the mending that I left on the chaise lounge for you. I expect it to be done when I get back."

I rushed to empty the bathwater—bucket after bucket. I shuffled back and forth to the rear yard until my back pained me to move. Field hands crossed the lower part of the yard. They sang a message loud enough for me to hear. It told that Calvin was waiting down at the river, sitting under the tulip tree. When I dumped the last bucket of water, I finished the laundry that I had left sitting not far from the well.

When the wash was done, I returned to the house and entered the missus' bedroom. My eyes widened; they filled with disbelief. My hands fumbled as I picked up the soiled clothing from Missus' bath time and dropped the pieces into the laundry basket. I could barely see any bit of the chaise lounge. It was buried beneath a heap of clothing: gowns, jackets, nightshirts, undershirts, dress shirts, skirts, pinafores, and trousers. A straw sewing basket crammed with collars and cuffs was on top of the batch. My heart flopped in the bottom of my stomach. I would never finish mending what I see in time to meet Calvin before the missus returned from her outing. My knees buckled to the floor. I crawled next to the mound of garments and braced my back against the chaise lounge. I pulled a dark red and green calico skirt from the batch, stretched it across my lap, and stared down on it. I held a needle up to the light to see through the eye of it. I pushed the thread toward the spark. As quickly as I could, I started hemming the skirt that blanketed my lap. I pricked one fingertip and then another. My tears washed away the blood droplets that surfaced. They fell on the skirt. I was glad the fabric was dark. Not much of the spotting showed.

My head jerked when the night bell rang. It let the hands know it was time for them return to the quarters. The sound conjured angry feelings in my gut. I yearned to be free from the ugliness of the life I was experiencing once more.

The next day I was still mending. After Angeline fed the chickens, collected eggs, and gathered herbs from the garden, she hurried to the big house. She ran up the stairs to Missus' bedroom. Winded, she plopped down and helped me hem, mend, and sew on buttons.

"My fingers be sore. I ain't never gonna meet Calvin down by the river. And he seems to be a good somebody to be gettin' to know. I be wantin' to talk to him. Ain't never had the chance to meet nobody. We keep being moved. Done lived with so many of these here Higgs.

One farm be lookin' like the next. Tell me again who you say own me when I's a wee one?"

"That be Master Reuben Higgs. We's also owned by Master Jacob, Miss Elizabeth, and Miss Wineford Amanda, and there was others. But we's here now. Don't be lettin' your mind be troubled with what's done passed. We got to make the best of what we got here."

"And here's where I be tryin' to meet that young buck. I might be wantin' to git to know him mo," I said with tears in my eyes.

"You be meetin' soon enough. Don't you cry, gal. No need to be sad."

"I won't be able to meet a soul if Missus don't stop heapin' this here work on me. It be so much, I ain't got time to visit with myself."

Angeline and I chuckled some and then we hugged. We kept sewing, and I kept weeping. It felt good to have my sister next to me.

The next day's sun came up and went down. More work was heaped on me before I was done with the job at hand. It continued like that for more days. I worked alone because Angeline had to return to her chores.

One late night in 1860, some days later and getting a bit warmer, the Higgs smothered the candlewicks and put out the oil lamps. They went to bed unusually early. That left me with a good amount of time to race down the carriage lane to meet Calvin under the tulip tree. I wasn't sure he'd be there.

A cool fall-like breeze came up off the river. It tempered the summer heat along its bank. I saw the top of the tulip tree just over the rise. It was weighed down with yellow blooms, each cupping an orange glow. Soon its floral sweetness greeted me. Calvin relaxed against the tree trunk, whittling on a small piece of wood. He had the look and voice of a good man.

A blush of giddiness warmed me as I watched his hands shave the chip.

"Calvin," I whispered from behind the tree.

"Been here every night waitin' for you," he said, not looking around. "I knowed you'd come sooner or later. Been makin' this here for you."

I circled the tree and stood in front of him. I didn't speak. I wasn't sure what to say. My insides quivered so I felt sickly.

"Since you here, go 'head and rest yourself," he said, patting the ground next to him.

I sat close to Calvin, but not close enough for our bodies to touch like I wanted them to. He turned himself and glanced at me. I looked away, unable to let my eyes be seen.

"When you in trouble, just blow it. I'll come, if I hear it."

"It be a mighty pretty little whistle. Fits nicely in my hand."

I rolled it over in my palm, fingered its

shape, and tapped the tiny holes. It was smooth and warm like the late sun on a hot day. I put it to my lips. Holding the whistle between them, I studied it before I blew into it.

"Got the sound of a songbird."

"Be like your voice," Calvin said.

After that evening, whenever Calvin and I could, we sat under the tulip tree. He held my hand. With his piney breath, he whispered sweet words in my ear. For hours we exchanged thoughts about how white folks stood in the way of slaves marrying properly. Then we chitchatted about the freedom we both craved, the mistreatment of slaves; and how we all suffered, field hands as well as house servants. We even chattered about runaways that escaped on the Underground Railroad, the howling and growling of the dogs that chased the barefoot scents, and the cries of those who were caught by the beasts. At times we chuckled about funny nothings. Our laughing tears fell at the expressed thoughts of Master Marcus being our slave, doing the washing, cooking, grooming us, and the missus nursing our babies.

Calvin and I eventually had our own baby gal. I named her Mona. My mind was troubled after her birth. I wanted Mona to grow up to be a proper lady whose able to read, write, and figure. She was my greatest joy, but I had to put her to sleep in a laundry basket when I worked. It pained me each time I gazed down at her sweet face, knowing I didn't have the proper minutes to hold her, kiss her plump cheeks, tickle her tiny toes, or rub noses when it's sleep time.

3

The Higgs' Estate

I didn't see much of Aaron and Angeline. They worked on the other side of the farm. We gathered most Sundays to visit and talk about our days.

It was four years later when I entered the big house to start my usual day's work. From the top of the stairs, I detected a great deal of commotion. It came from the big bedroom where Master Marcus normally slept. It seemed he had died. Master Wyly and his sister,

Missus Prudence, were at his side. They sat with him during his sickly days.

Not knowing what to do, I gathered the silver tea service to polish it. Visitors started coming and going right away. They brought food and their condolences day and night, even after the body was put in the ground. My chores around the house didn't keep my ears from taking in what was being said.

I knew, too, when someone in the Higgs family died, my brother Aaron, my sister Angeline, and I would be moved to another Higgs family estate. It didn't matter which Higgs household I belonged to; life for me was always hellish. My work could never be done: Do this. Do that. Keep moving. Don't stop the Higgs always yelped at me.

I pondered about which Higgs we'd go to, Master Wyly or Missus Prudence. They were the two Higgs children left. At one time there were four of them.

Master Wyly and Missus Prudence came to the house one day after Master Marcus was in the ground. They talked about who would get what. Sometimes they squabbled about how to divide the land and what to do with the nearly dozen slaves. Don't know which one said it, but someone said my baby and I were worth $1,400.00. Finally, It was decided that Master Wyly would get half of the slaves, including Aaron and Angeline. Miss Prudence would get the other half, along with me and my baby Mona.

I was down at the springhouse to get butter when I hears Aaron and Angeline screaming. They were being forced into the back of a wagon with other slaves. They leaned from the rear of it and cried out for me, yelling my name. Master Wyly slapped the rear of the horses and was off in a flash. My brother and sister and I reached for one another. No one heard my screams except my baby Mona.

She held tightly to my leg, sure that she was going to be snatched from me. I had never been separated from Aaron or Angeline, except when one of us was hired out to another farm owner.

After the wagon was out of sight, I grabbed Mona's hand and headed up the alley. I ran. My gal trotted at my side. Once inside the cabin, I closed the door, leaned against it, and struggled to catch my breath. In the pit of my stomach a fire hotter than the one in hell festered. Blazing so, it made me feverish and cold at the same time.

The empty cabins echoed a ghostly cry. I gathered logs and started a fire. I needed to chase the chill in the air. Afterward, I sat on the floor and moved close to the flames. Mona crawled underneath my skirt, wanting to hide from what scared her.

Miss Prudence married Master Albert L. Cheairs. They bought Master Wyly's half of the farm down at Grays Creek in Bolivar which is in the Southeastern part of Tennessee.

Miss Prudence and her new husband packed up the household. They moved the contents, along with Mona, me, and the other slaves to the family farm. Not enough could be said about the beauty of Gray's Creek, how it stretched along the waterway and smelled of country freshness. Beauty or no beauty, I couldn't imagine life, here or anywhere, without Aaron and Angeline.

A year later, 1861, when the Civil War started, I heard excitable snippets from the white folks' talk. They spoke of a man named Abraham Lincoln. They said he was president of the United States and wanted to end slavery in the North and the South, too.

The Southerners wanted to fight to keep their slaves. They advocated that "the economy of the South is dependent on slave labor to survive. Without it, we will perish."

Northerners rebutted by saying "it's an unfair labor practice and the time has come to put an end to the abuse."

The Northerners began forming a Union Army while Southerners continued to argue that the cotton had to be picked and bailed, rice patties harvested, and sugar cane processed– none of it could be done without the slaves. "Our livelihood depends on it" they said as they pushed to form the Confederate Army.

The two sides armed themselves with artillery. They aimed at each other and surged into battle. The Confederates fought the Union Army. They were determined to keep their slaves. Sons of the North and sons of South left home in staggering numbers. Brothers fought against brothers and fathers against sons.

Calvin and I spoke more frequently about how the two of us were fed up with life on the Higgs farm. It was time for me to run. I hoped it was for Calvin too. I had heard about and seen Negroes escaping. "Goin' to join the Union Army and fight with the colored troops" they said when they came upon Grays Creek.

Slaves at Gray's Creek sang about the freedom seekers that kept passing the farm on their way to Bolivar, Tennessee. The slaves who could read scavenged for thrown-away newspapers. Others walked among the white farm owners. Their attentive ears caught hold of and held onto words that revealed a war was going on to free the slaves in the North, as well as those in the South. Back at the quarters they shared what they learned and their longing to be free.

The talk of freedom made my ears burn, my skin tingle, and my legs wobble. My heart thudded excitedly. From day to day, I couldn't keep my mind on my work or what I needed to do. Sometimes I stood in the doorway of my cabin and listened to the songs that wafted up from the fields. They carried messages about the Underground Railroad, letting us know when it was coming through and telling us to be ready to get on board when it did. The singing made me anxious.

I heard more bits of news from the white folks as I sauntered through the big house, going out to the rear yard. The field hands were singing *Go Down Moses*, *Nobody Knows the Trouble I See,* and *Git on Board Little Chillen*." Not only did the songs tell about what was happening, but to be ready when the train comes through or to stay put. I was ready and wanting to run. I wanted to be free. I dreamed every minute of every day and night of not having to answer to the white man's call.

4

1862

I was about twenty-four years old and Mona nearly four, the war was in its second year. The number of runaways grew daily. Miss Prudence kept a closer than usual eye on the slaves at Gray's Creek. She assigned unreasonable jobs that could never be finished, ensuring that her slaves were too exhausted to run as far as the barnyard when the day ended.

Missus assigned me to fan her while she napped during the day and slept at night. At bedtime, she kept Mona with her. "To keep my feet warm" she said, knowing that I would never run and leave my baby behind.

One day in June of 1862, Miss Prudence and Master Albert were preoccupied with new furnishings that had arrived at the front door. The pieces were too large to fit through the yard door at the rear of the house. I rushed to my cabin. I pushed aside the bedding and the straw mounded on the pallet. From beneath it, I snatched up a burlap sack I had packed for the day that I would run. I trapped it in my armpit and scooped up Mona. Her arms clasped my neck. Her legs clamped to my waist. I squeezed her against me and crossed the fields, running and calling for Calvin. He came from behind a tree and slapped his plow-rough hand over my mouth.

"Gal, you gonna get us hung?"

"I's sorry, Calvin. But I's ready to go. I wants to be free. Now!" I said with my quiet yelling voice.

"You sure 'bout that?"

"Sure as the sky is blue and this here is my gal."

"You gotta wait. This ain't the time. I done heard eyes are on the lanes. Trails, too. Go on back to the big house. We gotta wait for the next sign."

I felt anger rise up inside me. I wanted to run. I wanted to run now! I pouted and stomped my way back up the carriage lane. I took my sack back to the cabin and went on to the big house. I worked, cleaning the front steps. Mona moved up and down each one with me. Missus smiled, glad she could keep an eye on me. When that job was done,

Missus had me clean her shoes. She had gone down to the creek and muddied them something awful. "Walking to get some fresh morning air" she said. Next thing I knew, I was on my knees scrubbing the floor and then scraping and polishing shoes.

Daylight faded and Missus sent for Mona. My legs and back cramped me so bad that I couldn't carry Mona up to the Missus' room. My gal caught hold of my skirt tail. I pulled her along with me until we were at the top of the staircase. I knocked on the bedroom door. When there was no answer to my call, I eased it open. I laid Mona against Missus' feet. She never acknowledged us. It was like this, day after day, seeming like weeks or maybe a lifetime. I was beginning to think I was gonna die before I woke from this dreadful nightmare.

One day, something unexpected occurred. Missus wanted to keep Mona with her for the day but changed her mind. So, I took Mona to the kitchen with me. She played with the spuds until it was time for me to cook them. I took the taters and gave her a fist full of walnuts and another full of pecans collected from the ground. She tossed and rolled them around the yard, laughing and pretending. She didn't seem to miss the potatoes.

Later that day, I stood in the middle of the rear yard. The summer weather had shed its humidity and stepped aside for the 1862 Fall season. I had just wrung a chicken's neck and held it by its legs. I waved at Calvin, who postured near the edge of the property with his hands on his hips. We both turned when we heard the thudding sound of crunching and rustling bare feet from behind the roadside trees. It's gotta be the train, I thought. Before I knew it, a party of dusty Negroes emerged from the thicket. They were running from their enslavers. With the chicken still in my hand, I rushed to meet them.

"Where you be goin'?" I asked them.

"We's marchin' North. Goin' to Bolivar, Tennessee. Gonna join up with the Union Army. Gonna be part of the colored troops."

I couldn't wait any longer. Train or no train, I knew my time was here. I glanced at Calvin. When he nodded his head, I ran back to the yard, tossed the chicken to one of the Negroes, and scampered off to the cabin. I grabbed the knapsack and hurried back to the yard. Mona was still playing with her make-believe frogs and birds. I picked her up. Quick as I swat a pesky fly, we joined Calvin, who waited at the alley for us. The three of us caught up with the Negroes on their way to join the colored army. Our group ran nearly three hard miles, seldom stopping to rest. With the twists and turns we took along the way, it could have been five. At least that's what it felt like to me.

It was more later than sooner when we reached Bolivar, Tennessee. Mona and I were separated from Calvin. The Union Army had recruited him for the colored troops. I was alone and frightened. When I looked around, I saw only a river of deep-blue coats decorated with gold buttons and pinched at the waist with a smart leather belt. I stood in a state of shock, not sure what to do. The cluster of blue coats seemed to swallow up Mona and me. I bowed my head and called on the Lord once more. That's when I heard voices and stopped praying to listen. I raised my eyelids just enough to see the feet clad in roughened cowhide boots surrounding me.

"Hey! Hey here! You're the Grand 23rd Indiana Volunteer Infantry Regiment of the

United States" I heard a voice say not far from my ears.

Raising my head a bit more, I saw the eyes of the soldiers who balanced caps on their heads. Not all of them were pleased to see me or my gal. Some behaved as if the smell of death had moved into the camp. Mona and I were contraband. I knew the danger that we were in. I turned my face away from the stares of the mean-spirited men.

The thought of the evil catchers coming after me made my aching body shiver from the kerchief on my head to the bottom of my blistered and bleeding feet.

Misery taunted me with hunger, footsoreness, cold, and fear the soldiers would hand me and my gal over when we were come for. If the soldiers give us to the catchers, they'd surely beat and lash me to near death before returning us to Grays Creek. Missus Prudence wouldn't hesitate to take Mona away from me and then order one of her unreasonable punishments such as a hundred lashes or to be locked in the dark with no food or water 'til my soul pleaded to go on to the next world. There's no mercy for runaways.

Feeling desperate and lonely, I begged the boys in the blue coats to let me wash their uniforms, mend their clothes, cook their meals, and care for them whenever they got the miseries. More than a few of the soldiers looked at me with doubtful eyes. One soldier made his way through the crowd. He carried a plate of beans and a tin cup filled with water.

"Go ahead. You and your pickaninny have yourselves some of this here. You look hungry and broken-down."

"Thank you kindly, sir."

Mona and I were given a corner of the yard where we could eat, rest, and later sleep. The soldiers who passed gaped at us. Some spoke. Some spit on us. Others just acted as if we weren't there.

Not sure what to make of Mona and me, one by one the soldiers began to allow me to wash a little something for them. Some gave me a small piece of game they had caught and needed cooking. As the days passed, I moved around the camp more freely. It wasn't long before I became the laundress for the 23rd Regiment. I mended uniforms and continued to cook for the soldiers. The ones who hadn't accepted us before, began to admire my work. Others talked and played with Mona—even strolled her around the grounds, holding her by the hand.

5

Slave Catchers

One day a group of strange men arrived at the encampment of the 23rd Regiment. I snatched up Mona, frightening her to tears. I pulled her into my bosom and covered her mouth to hush her cries. The two of us slipped in among the soldiers gathered to greet the loud, scrawny bunch of men. I hid as best I could for fear that they were slave catchers who had come to take Mona and me away. The men declared their business. "That nigress and her pickaninny need to be turned over to us at once" they told the soldiers.

My teeth clattered when the strangers demanded, with fingers pointing at Mona and me, that we were to be turned over to them without delay. I eased deeper into the sea of blue coats. Squatting low, with frightful tremors, I pleaded with the soldiers standing at my side.

"Please, sir, don't give us to them."

I crouched over Mona. The soldiers closed in around us. They created a human wall and refused to let the catchers take us.

"No," they said, again and again, each time with a firmer voice.

The soldiers stood at attention. Defeated, the catchers left. Mona and I remained with the 23rd Indiana Regiment. For the first time since I arrived at the camp, I was able to fill my lungs with air. I took in a breath so deep that my shoulders heaved up to my ears, capturing the peace that cloaked my entire being. I grinned, sure that I tasted granules of sweet freedom on the tip of my tongue. I thanked the men and scurried off, giddy with delight, to continue my chores. Along the way, I raised my chin and looked toward the sky. I thanked the Lord. "You done took care of me and my gal again." A smile broadened inside of me.

The morning after the slave catchers left, I sprang from my cot and kicked my foot up like I was gonna to do the Juba dance, but I didn't. Instead, I tied my hair up with a red and blue kerchief and pinned on a flour-sack apron with peace of mind.

That day I washed, ironed, sewed, mended, and cooked with the zest of a puppy. I cared for an ailing soldier and managed the wounds of another. I worked until I was happily exhausted. I was not a large woman, but I was robust in my sureness. I had a face some said was smooth and black as a spade. Yet, no one turned away from it. My dark cheeks radiated a quietness that settled uneasy souls who came within sight of them. The harshness that some of the men felt when I first arrived at camp melted like lard in a warm Dutch oven.

"Miss Lucy, I can hear your voice throughout the campgrounds . . . a calming tune, like the sound the wind makes when it brushes the tree leaves," one of the boys said to me when passing by. After I thanked him, he gave Mona a small doll he whittled for her. Filled with delight, I continued with my duties.

"Come! Come! I sew that button on for ya, sir. Come close, Massa. I stitch dat rip on ya sleeve. Let me fix ya some warm victuals. Sir, give me dat coat. I clean dat fa ya. I patch dat coat and dem trouser legs too," I offered.

When I was done sewing and mending, I took care of Mona and me. Some days I'd send the boys to fetch wild meat for a special meal.

"Bring me that lost turtle. I make you some terrapin soup and cornbread. Put that bacon down der. Pull me some of dem wild onions. I'll get dat chicken dat's peckin' at dat throw-away corncob."

There was little doubt that the fires flamed beneath my stewing pots were lit. The aroma escaped and wafted over the campgrounds, floating in and out of the men's tents. The soldiers gathered around my campfires. They knew I had extra for them. They held out tin cups. I filled each almost to the brim.

As time went on, the soldiers grew more protective of my baby Mona and me. We gave them the sense of family they had left behind. I never had trouble with the men that I couldn't handle on my own. They stopped calling me Miss Lucy and started calling me Aunt Lucy.

6

Healing Hands

From the corner of my eye, I saw Dr. Magnus Brucker. He was the head surgeon for the 23rd Regimental unit. He had been watching me from a distance since the sun came up. It wasn't because I was the only colored and the only woman in the unit; no one seemed to notice those details anymore.

Dr. Brucker studied my hands. He noted that his men responded favorably to me and showed a great deal of respect. They never called me what I shouldn't be called or put their hands on me where they shouldn't be put.

Dr. Brucker flagged me toward him with a wide-casting arm.

"Come, Lucy. I want to speak with you," he hollered.

I quickly handed the plate of victuals to a soldier nearby. He continued feeding his ailing mate. I hurried across the yard to where the doctor stood.

"You be needin' me, sir?"

"I do. You've been taking mighty good care of these men. They're fond of you. You have an enabling manner and gentle touch. Your quiet voice is soothing, for sure. The men refer to you as Miss Lucy. Some call you Aunt Lucy."

"Sir, they don't mean no harm. I just be tryin' to make them feel some easiness from their loneliness and the hurtin' they been feelin', along with their wounds. Please, sir, don't be upset with the men. I won't cause no trouble."

"Take care, Lucy. No harm's been done. I like the way you nurture the men and how they respond to you. I want you to be our hospital nurse. That is, if you'd like to."

"I'd be mighty proud to work for you, sir. And mighty pleased to nurse them boys and serve the 23rd."

"You'll be paid well for your services."

I didn't think about the money at first. And if Dr. Brucker had said something more, I didn't hear it. My gut was so crammed with happiness, I dropped to my knees. I swayed back and forth. Without thought, I clamped my joyous arms around Dr. Brucker's leg. He laid a gentle hand across my back and took me by the arm. With ease, he pulled me to my feet.

"Go on back to your quarters. Your work for today is done. Don't worry about the soldiers you were helping. I'll send someone to finish your work. Go on and prepare for tomorrow.

You'll need your rest. You'll be rising with the rooster, and he crows early. Your hours will be long, and the work won't be easy."

"That be fine, sir. I be gittin' on my way. I be back. I be on time, too."

I prepared an early supper of rice, beans, and cornbread for Mona and me. When we were done eating, I drew the night cover over us, even though the day was still full of brightness. Mona didn't sleep until after several songs, stories, and make-believes. I was certain I'd never sleep. I wondered if I would get the money that Dr. Brucker promised.

When sleep came, I dreamed I was putting a new comb in my hair and tying pretty ribbons in Mona's. Then I saw myself tucking a fancy doll in bed with her and reading a store-bought book to her when I didn't know how to read. Wearing a crisp Sunday dress, Mona slipped her feet into a new pair of shiny shoes. All of this, while we stood in Glory Land and drank from the dipper of sweet freedom with time to play, time to rest, time to love, and time for all to pray. My brain fish-flopped through the night with no end to wishing, wanting, and hoping. I even heard Angeline's voice in my head, "One day you gonna be a fine lady, like you always dreamed of. I been prayin' it for you. And it's gonna be so."

At 4:00 a.m. the next morning, the rooster crowed. My heavy eyes were pulled open by the fowl's cry. I never knew when I fell asleep. I sat straight up and pulled my boots on one at a time. I laced them with exactness and tucked the strings inside the rims. I finger-combed my hair and then knotted it up in a white kerchief. I pinned on a freshly pressed flour-sack apron and tied a perfect bow at the rear. I loaded Mona, still sleeping, in my arms.

Dr. Brucker was waiting at the opening of the hospital tent. "Inside are your men. They need you," he told me as he stepped aside so

Mona and I could enter.

I bowed my head with a slight curtsey toward Dr. Brucker as I entered the tent. Nothing more needed to be said.

I laid Mona on a vacant cot. The air in the hospital tent was foul. It was consumed with the smells of filth, rotting flesh, sickness, and soiled bodies. When I stepped over a pile of amputated arms, legs, and other body parts, I gripped my gut to hold my innards down. I didn't look back. I went right to work. I cared for the men as if I had been their personal nurse since the beginning of the war. I hurried to give attention to a young soldier whose cries drew me toward him. I squeezed his forearm to stop the bleeding from a deep flesh wound. He tried to jerk away, but I held on to his arm.

"You get the doctor. I don't want your black hands on me."

"The doctor is taking off a bad leg. If you don't quiet down, he'll be taking off your arm. I take care to use only the white side of my hands. You rest easy now."

When the boy slipped out of consciousness, I cleaned his wound and bandaged his arm. Then I turned to another soldier. I took out my pocket knife that I used to skin rabbits with and dug a bullet out of his leg. I dressed his wound and then checked the wounds of others.

A couple of hours later, the soldier with the slashed arm woke up. He realized he still had his arm, and the pain was not as troubling. He gave me a shame-faced stare that I pretended not to notice.

"How you feelin', sir? You Jon Boy, ain't you?"

"I am. And I be sorry. Didn't mean no harm the way I talked to you. Wasn't no cause for it," the soldier said and closed his eyes, not able to look into mine.

"You rest. I be back to make sure that arm's healin' good."

"Miss Lucy, I thank you for what you did for me."

I tucked Jon Boy's covers around his neck and chest. Then I continued caring for the other sick and injured: adjusting soiled dressings, changing beddings, cleaning up sickness, combing matted hair, feeding whoever needed to be fed, giving medications, and putting fresh dressings on bleeding wounds. I did whatever I needed to do to help the soldiers return to their duties. I worked hard and long into the night. When Mona and I finally left the hospital tent, we strolled beneath a bright pearly moon that lit the footpath. The dark sky was stuffed with winking stars.

I was tired, hungry, and exhausted but bloated with joy. I fed Mona more of yesterday's beans and cornbread. She washed it down with fresh goat milk. I put her to bed. Then I ate the same. When I lay stretched out on the cot with my body close to hers, I sank with weariness, but peace was at hand. I woke early the next morning, 'fore the rooster crowed. I couldn't wait to see the men. I knew the boys looked forward to my coming and caring for them. I never missed a day and was never late.

7

The Battles

The 23rd Regiment spent most of the 1862 Summer in Bolivar, Tennessee. It was detailed for outpost duty. I watched men come and go until I couldn't count them, keep up with them, or know all their names. My work doubled, maybe tripled. I stopped figuring the number of skirmishes that popped up. By the time I bandaged one soldier, the horse-drawn ambulance delivered another, laying him out for me to fix before leaving to fetch the rest of his comrades. I worked sun up to sun down and up and down again.

It was the first part of September 1862 when the taps sounded to let the 23rd Regiment know that it was time to pack up and move out. The soldiers loaded war goods such as food rations, tents, medical supplies, and other stocks onto horseback to be transported to the station. With Mona braced on my hip, I followed the blue coats. I walked slowly at first. The thunder of boots passed me on both sides. *Chip-chop. Chip-chop. Chip-chop.* The boots were heard far and near. I increased my pace until my boots gave off a profound cadence. I marched proudly with the boys in blue. Like theirs, my head was up and my back straight with squared shoulders.

We boarded a train and traveled by rail to Jackson, Mississippi. From there, the men participated in more battles and skirmishes. I was at the rear of the movement, taking care of the wounded. One day was the same as the next; marching, marching more; nursing, and nursing more. I was seldom sure of where I was, except when I was in the trenches.

During October, the 23rd Regiment, along with a number of other regiments, were in pursuit of Ripley, Mississippi. Before I knew it, I had marched 52 miles southward in 48 hours. I know because I heard some of the men grumblings when I wrapped their feet. The regiments were attempting to get to Vicksburg, but the supplies were damaged, and the effort failed. The troops, fatigued and worried, returned to Memphis, Tennessee.

When fall 1862 rushed in and then out, the days were interrupted by one of the worst winter seasons ever. The snow was heavy, roads were nearly impassable, and provisions were limited. For ten days we scavenged for food, picking field peas when we could find them. I was always cold, hungry, and numb for too many days. I couldn't feel all my body parts. My feet and fingers ached. They were slow to move when I bandaged or fed the injured. With the supplies being so scarce, taking care of the boys wasn't easy. Each day became more difficult to live. I was constantly tired from a lack of proper sleep.

By Christmas Eve we had reached the *Yocknapatafa River in Mississippi. Our rations were severely depleted. We were issued ordinary dry corn. Many of the soldiers frowned while some popped it on hot ash. I smiled. The corn took my mind back to when I was a young gal not much higher than Mammy's knee. I gripped onto a rock and did what I used to do– grind corn kernels into a fine mill. I boiled the ground peas and the weeds I had gathered and squashed it together with the cornmill. I didn't have much fat or salt to give it the usual taste. I pinched and rolled clumps of the mixture into

*Yocknapatafa River, as noted in Shadrach K. Hooper, First Lieutenant and Adjutant, "Historical Sketch of the 23rd Indiana Volunteer Infantry"

walnut-sized balls. Afterward, I flattened them into small round cakes and dropped them on the hot ash. The fire sparked good memories.

I set some of the ashcakes near the fire for Jon Boy, like I had promised him I would. I glanced at my baby, Mona. She had grown thin, pale, and weak. I told her about when I's a young gal like her and gathered around the fire with the old mammies. Bent over, they sang in sweet voices, humming like songbirds as they worked. I remember how clear their words were:

> *Swing low, sweet chariot,*
> *Comin' for to carry me home . . .*

They made little treats like this. I showed Mona what I held in my hand. Ashcakes, we called them. We gobbled them up so fast, you never knowed if they were ever on the hot fire or not.

Feeling joy, I chuckled for a split second as I told my story. When Mona didn't respond, a sadness slipped in. It consumed me. My gal's face was more sunken than an old man's whose eyes were near to blindness. I gently pulled her into the folds of my dress. I draped her in all the warmth I had. With my fingers, I fed her ashcakes moistened with the boiled weeds. I rocked her slackened body. I sang *Swing low, sweet chariot* to her like Mammy did for me. My baby stared at me but didn't seem to see me or hear my singing voice. My tears refused to stay put. They fell onto Mona's cheek. I pushed them aside and pulled her closer to me. Although I felt a deep sadness inside me, I thanked the Lord that I had her. Just then, Jon Boy came by. I nodded my head toward the fire and he picked up his ashcakes.

"Can I sit here with you to eat my cakes?"

"Sho you can."

Jon Boy moved in close to me. He held onto the ashcakes, studying them. I sensed his fear and pain.

"Go on. It be okay, boy. You go head and eat," I said to him with a reassuring voice and a pat on his leg.

Jon Boy nibbled the crisp edges of his cakes.

"Aunt Lucy, sometimes you seem full of joy when the rest of us are struggling to smile. I notice you chuckling when I can't laugh. What were you thinking about at those moments?"

Beaming and rocking Mona, I said, "I was thinkin' about a lot. One of them things was about the day Mona and me was walking behind the wagon train. I's a talkin' and a laughin' with Mona, but my legs be tired and my feet be startin' to feel some soreness. I's singin' to her when one of the soldiers inside the wagon–don't remember who– said, 'Aunt Lucy, let me give you and that youngun of yours a ride.' That was a good day, Jon Boy. I think those things 'cause they give me hope. You got to find you a good day and think about it."

"Mine was the day when you saved this

here arm." Jon Boy said. Then he scooted closer and rested his head on my shoulder.

The time spent in Tennessee was brutal. The overcrowded zig-zag trenches were cold, damp, dirty, and full of troublesome odors. No matter which way I looked, the earth was blood-stained. The cold temperatures and lack of food were vexing too. Bad things didn't seem to have an end. I worried about Mona. I couldn't keep her warm. I didn't even have body heat to give her.

Some days later, the much-needed rations and supplies arrived at camp. The 23rd was able to march on to Collierville, Tennessee, and then Memphis, and back and forth to Vicksburg, Mississippi.

Each time we got to Vicksburg, I searched for Calvin. I wanted to know if he was well and unharmed. I called out for him and blew the whistle he made for me. A voice told me he's done gone on. Another soldier said Calvin joined the foot soldiers, and still another said he had been killed. I didn't know which news was true, but felt certain Calvin had gone on, to where, I wasn't sure. But I knew for sure I was alone and my heart ached. I didn't complain about my loss. The men in blue needed me and I needed to be strong. I concealed my feelings and continued taking care of the soldiers.

The May 18th and May 22nd attacks on Vicksburg led to the Saturday, July 4, 1863, surrender by the Confederate soldiers. The 23rd Regiment was there to receive it. I was among the men. That was one time that I remembered the month, day, and year. I was also there when they got the award for their service and the surrender.

Shortly after that, Mona fell ill. Her lips were cracked; her nose was red and runny. She was congested and coughed constantly. Her flesh grew to be fire hot. I couldn't feel the weight of her body against me. One night when I was cradling her in my lap, I dozed off. When I wasn't paying attention, she slipped away with the angels. My tears wouldn't stop flowing. My anguish couldn't be contained.

The men of the 23rd took Mona from my grip. They had grown fond of her. She was the little gal they cared about and watched over. The boys in blue mourned the loss of their bright-eyed, perky friend. They dug a tiny grave. With heavy hearts, the boys covered Mona's body with tiny wildflowers. All I had to give her was the whistle that Calvin carved for me. I tied it around her neck. When she gets to heaven, she can blow it. If Calvin hears it, he will answer her call.

Mona's wee body was lowered into a trench on the hillside, above the city, close to the angels. They are her guardians now and will watch over her for me.

Standing at the graveside, squeezing wildflowers, their capped heads were bent in prayer. The boys in blue recited a Bible verse. Afterward, they sang a sweet song of praise and then stood silent. The young soldiers were somber as they ambled away from the grave and back down the steep hill to their post.

My heart was strained once more. First, it was my brother Aaron and sister Angeline who were taken from me, and then Calvin going off. Now it's my baby Mona whose body was hard, cold, and buried alone in the ground.

I gathered my strength. From where I didn't know. But I did know that I needed to continue marching with the boys in blue. I carried on. Mona never once left my thoughts. I continued with my nursing duties, giving medication, bathing the filth from battered bodies, and spoon-feeding the sick. I tended to the battle wounds and never blinked an eye when I dressed a mangled limb or bandaged flesh that dangled from its bone. I couldn't count the many hours that I sat at their bedsides. I let my best ears listen to the concerns of the soldiers. They whimpered and talked out of their heads. I spoke quietly to temper the turmoil inside their heads. When they cried out for loved ones, I was there. I was the . . .:

> Buddy who helped them stay alive.
>
> Fiancé who comforted them.
>
> Girlfriend who supported their dreams.
>
> Mother who cradled their souls.
>
> Sister who listened to them.
>
> Wife who loved them.

I was whoever my boys needed me to be. "Acting like the angel . . . ," said Major Hooper.

The 23rd Regiment continued its duties in the Vicksburg, Mississippi. They were in the area until their August 28th furlough. The men had completed their three-year commitment with the regiment. Some of them were glad to be going home to their loved ones, most re-enlisted. I was pleased for the opportunity to steal snippets of time away from my duties to rest and think about Mona, Calvin, Aaron, and Angeline.

The regiment went on to New Albany, Indiana, maybe to Louisville, Kentucky. Sometimes I get things mixed up, but I know for sure I stayed and moved on with the 23rd when I could have left them. But I had no family to go to. The men in blue were my family now.

After the furlough, I continued to trudge along with them. We trotted until March 1864 when they had another month-long furlough. At the end of it, they fought more battles and skirmishes. It seemed some days that I'd never stop patching them up.

On Monday, April 10, 1865, when the 23rd Regiment packed up, the war was over. We easy-marched from North Carolina to Virginia and then on to Washington, D.C. The Grand Review was

Tuesday, May 23rd, and Wednesday. The next day, May 24th, we joined nearly 150,000 other parading soldiers who fought in the war. The procession passed the capital and then the viewing stands. They were crammed with great commanders. I'll never forget the good wishes called out to us from the reviewing politicians, officials, and prominent citizens, including President Andrew Johnson. The cheers were so loud I couldn't hear the *chip-chop* of the heavy boots next to me. It was the drummers who kept us in step. The Grand Review was a celebration that I never could have imagined and will never forget. The memory is held so deep inside of me, that I hardly know where I've tucked it. The only thing that could have made the day better was if Aaron, Angeline, Calvin, and my baby, Mona were at my side. They weren't, but I felt their spirits as if they were there with me.

8

After the War

When the ceremony ended, the men of the 23rd Regiment once more made an easy march. This time it was south to Louisville, Kentucky. We remained there for three months, resting and working until we were mustered out. There were no more battles and no more killings. The *chip-chop* faded and was heard no more. The men that were leaving for New Albany, Indiana, gathered around me.

"Aunt Lucy, we're going home. We want you to come along with us."

I didn't have a family or a place to call home. I was separated from my brother and sister since before the war. Calvin disappeared not long after we left Gray's Creek to join the colored army. My baby was buried at Vicksburg. The boys in blue were all the family that I had. I took a good look at them. I smiled inside and out, giggled some, and then said, "I be mighty pleased to go home with you."

New Albany was unwelcoming to a lot of Negroes at that time, but I was accepted and respected by most of the town's people. I became a citizen and was known as Aunt Lucy to most, the same as I had been to the boys of the 23rd Regiment.

It wasn't long after me arrived in New Albany that I went to work for the officers from the 23rd Regiment. Major Cooper's family was one of the first to hire me. I was with him and his family for a number of years before I left to work for Mr. W.Q. Gresham who was a neighbor that lived not far from the Cooper family. Mr. Gresham became Secretary of State. His family was so fond of me, I was asked to their daughter's wedding. I traveled with them to Chicago, Illinois. While there, I was an invited guest to the Palmer House. It was a huge hotel with paintings on the wall, high ceilings, wide columns, and a stairway like none I had ever seen before. Its beauty made my head spin. While I was there, I met some of the most well-known people in the United States.

The wedding was an elaborate affair. Women dressed in brocade, polished cotton, satin, and silk. The gowns were full of ruffles, tucks, and pleats. The plummeting necklines were stitched with lace. The women who wore bonnets secured them with wide puffy bows and adorned them with feathers, flowers, and ribbons. The men dressed in fine suits, some with tails. Their shirts had starched collars and cuffs and were accented with bow ties.

The meat was skewered and cooked over open fires. Its charred aroma was noticed throughout the neighborhood. Tables were crammed with food so fancy I could hardly eat it. In the large hall, the music excited me. I couldn't stop my feet from tapping and my heart from racing. The men on the dance floor held their ladies at the waist with fresh white hankies in their hands. They swirled their partners around. The fancy hooped skirts swooshed about. I found myself thinking about Calvin and the times he came courting me.

I kept everything I saw and heard in my head as I packed my grip for my trip back home. I beamed when they were visions of the elegant wedding and the various celebrations that took place. They sashayed in and out of my mind freely, leaving me with a light-headed feeling.

It was some years later when I fell sick with smallpox. The people who noted my illness never sent to the pesthouse where the other folks, which were diseased, were sent to be cared for and usually died.

One of the families from the 23rd Regiment took me in as if I were family and prepared a room for me. The boys took turns took care of me just as I had for them when they were sick and ailing.

On my trips to town, after I was well, some said, "Aunt Lucy, you one of the most well-known persons living here in New Albany."

Those city people, along with the boys from the 23rd, saw to it that I had a house to live in. It was a small two-story on Naghel Street. From there I took in laundry. Sometimes I nursed the sick.

In 1866, I became an honorary member of the William Standerson Post of the Grand Army of the Republic. GAR they called it. For many years I traveled 50 miles by rail from New Albany, Indiana, to English, Indiana, to attend the reunions. I never missed one that was in New Albany. At each meeting, the officers of the 23rd Regiment escorted me as if I were a queen. The roll was called by the secretary of the GAR: J.H. Curtis, F.M. Griggs, W. McClurie, J.D. Watts, W.W. Smith, and many more. Then I heard, "Lucy Higgs," and later, "Lucy Nichols." My chest rose with pride each year I heard my name called out. I scurried to my feet as if I had never heard it announced in such a way before.

"Here," I said, with musical notes caroling from my throat.

In 1870, at the age of thirty-two years, I married a man named John Nichols. He was a fine person. John and I worked hard to have a comfortable life together. Although he served in the army, he never received a pension. We didn't have much money. Life was hard, but at times, it was good. No children came from our 40 years together.

Word reached me that Congress had passed a special act allowing war nurses to apply for pensions. By then it was 1892. I was a 54-year-old housekeeper in diminishing health, but I felt sure I was qualified for such a pension. During the war, I was hired by Dr. Magnus Brucker to serve the regiment as a nurse. He promised me the day he gave me the job that I would be paid for the work that I did. I never received as much as a raccoon's foot. With the help of the men from the 23rd Regiment, I filed an application to request a pension. It revealed my history as a war nurse with the 23rd Indiana Volunteer Infantry Regiment. Congress rejected it, not once, but again and again.

There was no doubt that the men of the 23rd Regiment cared deeply about my quest. They remembered when I nursed them. "Aunt

Lucy, your hand was cold when it needed to be cold, It tempered my feverish brow," they told me.

Another said, "Your hand was warm when it needed to be warm. It soothed my shivering body."

Jon Boy said, "Your hand was firm when it needed to be firm. It stopped my arm from bleeding."

9

The Men Spoke Out

(No words or spellings have been changed.)

In 1894, George Moore, a Special Examiner from the U.S. Pension Office, was sent by the government to take depositions. Fifty-five of the men from the 23rd Regiment gave statements, telling how they knew me as Lucy Higgs and Lucy Nichols, and how I cared for them and the other men.

1 April, 1894, Dr. W. A. Burney

I am 47 years old; I have practiced medicine a little over 16 years, and my post office address is New Albany, Floyd Co., Ind. I graduated at Long Island College Hospital, Brooklyn, N.Y. I have known claimant at least 12 or 14 years, and have been her family physician off and on during that time. She has been and is now troubled with quinsy of the throat, and also asthma. She also has [. . .] attacks of trouble with the bowls, and those attacks are very debilitating during which time she is confined to her bed, and is not able to work at all. I also recall the fact that I have treated her for rheumatism in the elbow and shoulder joint. With all these troubles combined, she is not able to make her living by manual labor. From my observation she is quite poor [. . .]. I have understood your questions and my answers are correctly recorded.

William . A. Burney, M.D.

12 April 1894, Lorenzo D. Emory

I am a 52 years old; I am a carpenter by trade; and my post office address is New Albany, Floyd Co., Ind. I inlisted in Co. K 23 Ind. Vols. at New Albany, Ind. in June 1861, and I was mustered out in July 1865, at Indianapolis, Ind. Lucy Higgs now Lucy Nichols came to our regiment about July, 1862; her home was at Bolivar, Tenn. Dr. Brucker took her into the hospital there, and she wash, cooked for, and nursed the sick soldiers [. . .] She was a good nurse, and was with the regiment at Vicksburg, and Atlanta, Savanna, and onto Washington City, and then to Indianapolis, Ind. where she was

inlisted when we were mustered out.
I was orderly for the Doctor about 8
months, and had charge of the
ambulance, and I was in the hospital
[. . .], and she was there all the
time, and nursing the sick. [. . .]

I had a case of typhoid fever and
measles. [. . .]

I have understood your questions and
my answers are correctly recorded.
I am not interested in this claim.

Lorenzo . D. Emory

12 April, 1894, Charles E. Villier

I am 51 years old; I am a farmer and
my post office address is New
Albany, Floyd Co., Indiana. I inlisted
at New Albany, Ind. on June12,
1861 in Co. D 23 Ind. Vol. Inf. and
was mustered out July [. . .], 1864
at Indianapolis, Ind. I got acquainted
with Lucy Higgs now Lucy Nichols
at Bolivar, Tenn. In June, 1862

[. . .] she got into the hospital and acted as nurse for the 23 Ind. vols. [. . .] I think she got in the hospital under the Regimental Surgeon at Bolivar [. . . .]. After the surrender of Vicksburg, I was in the hospital there [. . .] with intermittent fever, and she was there waiting on us— making up the beds, and nursing and taking care of the sick and wounded soldiers [. . .] up to May, 1864, at which time I was takin sick [. . .].

Charles, E. Villier

13 April,1894, Benjamin F. Welker

I am 57 year-old; I am an attorney, and notary republic, and my post office address is New Albany, Floyd Co., Ind. I inlisted in Co. C. 23 Ind. Vol. Inf. at new Albany, Ind., on July 27, 1861 [. . .] I first knew Lucy Higgs or Nichols at Bolivar, Tenn. in summer of 1862. [. . .] I went to the hospital, and Dr. Magnus Brucker Chief Regimental Surgeon of the 23, Ind. told me he had employed Lucy Higgs as regular regimental nurse. [. . .] I was sick in the regimental hospital and claimant [. . .] took care of me in easy way that was a nurses duty to. [. . .] She was a success–an excellent nurse; I often heard the doctor say he did not know how he could get along without the assistance of claimant. She always knew what to do, and was attentive and ready. [. . .] I was postmaster for the regiment, and in carrying mail through the hospital I would see claimant there, and would [. . .] ask her where to find sick soldiers.

Benjamin F Welker

13 April, 1984, John Sandlawick

I am 60 years of age; I am flagman [. . .] my post office address is New Albany, Floyd Co. Ind. I inlisted in Co. A 23 Ind. Vols. during the War at New Albany, Ind. in 1861, and I was mustered out 1864 in Georgia. Lucy Nichols or Lucy Higgs came to the regiment at Bolivar, Tenn., about June, 1862. She washed for the regiment first and then she was put in the hospital to cook for and wait on the sick. Dr. Brucker took her into the hospital at Bolivar while we were camped there. Dr. Brucker is now dead. [. . .] Dr. Brucker employed her to attend to the sick and wounded. [. . .] The regiment [. . .] told me that claimant came home with them and went back when they went back.

I am not interested in this claim. I have understood your questions and my answers are correctly recorded.

John Sandlawick

♦♦♦

None of the depositions given by the former soldiers were enough to sway Congress. It made me angry that the U.S. Government ignored my services. I took it upon myself to write to the examiner at the Pension Bureau. With the help of the men from the 23rd Regiment, I scribed a letter. I couldn't read or write.

(No words or spellings have been changed.)

I am about 51 or 52 years old; I am a housekeeper, and my post office address is New Albany Floyd Co., Ind. I am the identical Lucy Nichols who claims pension as nurse during the War of the Rebellion. I claim pension under the Act of August 5, 1892. Dr. Brucker employed me as nurse at Bolivar, Tenn. I went to the regiment-23 Indiana in 1862, and was employed by Dr. Brucker to nurse the sick and wounded soldiers of that regiment–the 23 Regiment of Ind. Vols. of the United States Army. Dr. Brucker was the regimental surgeon. Dr. Byrn was also a surgeon; he left us after the surrender at Vicksburg, Miss. He now lives at Marengo, Ind. Dr. Brucker is now dead; he lived at Tell City, Ind. We went from Bolivar, Tenn. to Corinth, Miss and the regiment got into a skirmish there and then fell back, and we took our old camp again at Bolivar, Tenn. Then we staid there awhile, and then we went to Grenada and Holly Spring, Miss. Then we went to different places in Mississippi, and across to Atlanta, Ga.

and to the Sea–at Beaufort, S. C. Then through Virginia to Washington City, D. C. We camped there awhile, and from there we went to Indianapolis, Ind. and we were mustered out at Indianapolis.

After Vicksburg surrendered, the regiment was furloughed for 60 days, and I came home with them, and went back with them. I was with the regiment during the whole time from Bolivar, Tenn. to Indianapolis, Ind. I served as nurse about 3 years. I cooked for the soldiers, dressed their wounds, gave them medicine, and washed for them, and did anything I was called on to do. I served in the hospital at Bolivar, Tenn. I serve under the name of Lucy Higgs and since the war I have married John Nichols–hence the name of Lucy Nichols. I have no documents showing that I was employed or discharged.

Dr. McPheeters of Hardinsburg, Ind. and Dr. Byrn of Marengo, Ind. had charge of the hospital at Bolivar, Tenn. They will remember my services. Lorenzo D. Emory, Charles Villier and B. F. Welker were members of the regiment and the 23 Ind. and he will remember me. John Hoffman. Hendersonville, Clark Co., Ind. Also knows of my serving as nurse. I am not able to earn support on account of having bronchitis and quinsy most all of the time, and I have been sick and under treatment of a physician all the winter. Dr. Burney has been my physician. I work some but I cannot work much; I am compelled to work to make something to live. My husband served in the army, but he does not receive a pension and has never applied for one. I have no children that served in the army.

I never received a nickel for my service as nurse; Dr. Brucker told me I would get paid, and I worked on in the hope of getting pay after a while. I was not under Miss Dorothea L. Dix. I was never in any hospital, but that of the 23rd Ind. Vols., and was with them till I was relieved at Indianapolis.

Lucy Nichols (X, her mark)

I signed my letter with a big "X", but telling my story in writing didn't sway the government. The application process continued six more years.

10

Six Years Later

*The 55th **Congress** – 2nd Session – House of Representative, Report No. 1397 – Lucy Nichols*
May 23, 1898

(These were their words.)

Her service and employment is not denied, but her application was denied at the Bureau because she was not employed by the authority recognized by the War Department as having such power [. . .]. About fifty odd soldiers who know of her valuable service join in asking this relief [. . .]. The number of said claim, which was rejected, for the reason on the ground that the records failed to show that she was employed as such nurse by proper authority for the period of six months. She feels aggrieved at said rejection [. . .] as she did serve as such nurse for a period of more than six months by authority of the chief surgeon [. . .] she files this her petition and prays your honorable bodies to pass a special act granting her a pension of $12.00 per month as she is now 60 years of age and in failing health.

In the matter of application of Lucy Nichols for special pension act as hospital nurse personally came before me [. . .]. Dr. A. Burney declares he has been her family physician during the most of *the time and especially during the last eight to ten years and treated her for [. . .] : Chronic rheumatism and chronic dyspepsia. Her rheumatism affected the arms and shoulder joints, causing them to be stiff and very painful on movement; also the back and hips and lower palpitation of heart and chronic constipation [. . .] these diseases [. . .] render her unable to perform manual labor [. . .].*

◆ ◆ ◆

It wasn't until 1898, that Congress had a hearing to pass a special act to honor my pension. It passed, but not without numerous challenges and hurdles.

Wednesday, December 14, 1898, I was granted my pension of $12.00 a month, along with my backpay. By then I was 60 years old.

That Christmas, I requested an audience with the men of the GAR. Commander A. R. Sharp sounded the alarm, calling the men in from their work. I waited in the outer chambers with an extra-large cake in hand. I was escorted down the aisle in a queenly way, the same as they did for me at our anniversary meetings. I presented my gift to the men. The cake and I were well received. It was a confection suitable for a royal family.

Even with my failing health, I continued to live in my small house. When I was 72 years old my husband John Nichols passed away. As time went on, I grieved, grew older, more feeble, and was no longer able to travel to the GAR gatherings. At the last meeting that I did attend, the boys prayed that the years to come would deal gently with me.

Jon Boy told the members of the GAR "Aunt Lucy is 77 years old now. She can't live alone. She can't look after herself any longer.

Aunt Lucy needs help with her personal needs and nearly everything else."

Not long after that, Jon Boy had to tell his fellow comrades, "On Monday, January 4, 1915, Aunt Lucy was taken to the Floyd County Poor House. Twenty-five days later, Friday, January 29, 1915, she died and was put to rest the next day." Jon Boy dabbed the tears that had fallen down his face before he went on to say, "I, like most of you and the town's people, loved and admired Aunt Lucy. She was the only woman member of the Grand Army. I'm glad she was buried with full military honors next to her husband, John Nichols. There is no tombstone and no marker. Only her grave. I can still hear the marching of the boots she always talked about, *"Chip-chop. Chip-chop. Chip-chop,"* as she moves toward the heavenly campground to join her baby Mona; her husband, John; her brother, Aaron; sister Angeline; and Calvin, the first man that was a part of her life."

The End

DISCUSSION QUESTIONS

1. How was Lucy's enslavement different from that of other slaves, whose stories you are familiar with?

2   If you could talk with Lucy, what would you say to her?

3. Should Lucy have endangered Mona's life by running away? Was it worth it?

4. Why were the soldiers protective of Lucy? What events occurred that let you know how much she was respected by the 23rd Regiment soldiers?

5. What was the pivotal point in Lucy's life?

6. What would have kept Lucy from running?

7. What were your thoughts when Lucy was separated from her brother and sister?

8. Did the fact that Lucy was never sold make her life any better? If so, why? If not, why not?

9. To what extent did Lucy go to show her depth of love for the boys in blue?

10. Lucy was an enslaved person who became a war nurse and then, a U. S. citizen. What were your feelings about these events in Lucy's life?

11. How would you describe Lucy's return to New Albany after the war to live with the 23rd Regiment?

12. What did it mean to Lucy when she got her pension?

13. Did Lucy have a good ending to her life?

14. Did Lucy deserve to be buried with full military honors?

SUGGESTED READING

Title: *The Daily Life of Susie King Taylor, Civil War*
Author: Margaret Gay Malone, editor

Title: *A Separate Battle: Women and the Civil War*
Author: Ina Chang

Title: *Taylor Reminiscences*
Author: Susan King Taylor

Title: *A Black Woman's Civil War Memoirs*
Author: Susan King Taylor

Title: *The Diary of Susie King Taylor*
Editor: Margaret Gay Malone

Title: *Diary of Susie King Taylor*
Author: Susie King Taylor

Title: *Mary Eliza Mahoney & The Legacy of African American Nurses*
Author: Susan Muaddi Darraj

ACKNOWLEDGMENTS

Carnegie Center for Arts and History, New Albany, Indiana, granted me opportunities to present The Life of Lucy Higgs Nichols, an interpretive program, to the families, friends, students, and supporters from their community.

First readers of the *Miss Lucy: Slave and Civil War Nurse* manuscript, made the publication possible.

Frazier History Museum, Louisville, Kentucky allowed me to take the stage to portray the story of Lucy Higgs Nichols to Jefferson County School children.

j. camille cultural academy, Louisville, Kentucky, staff members and partners diligently worked on my behalf, enabling me to write, *Miss Lucy: Slave and Civil War Nurse,* and continue with my work as the director of the *j. camille cultural academy*.

Laura Van Fossen, Civil War Education Day, Harrison County Courthouse Grounds, Corydon, Indiana, extended a repeated invitation for me to preform an interpretive program for the local students, community members, and the Civil War enthusiasts of Corydon, Indiana.

National Park Service, Underground Railroad Network to Freedom, supported my efforts and recognized my first-person interpretive programs .

Women Who Write, Louisville, Kentucky, members stood behind my work, encouraged me to pursue my writer's dream and never waffled on their support for me.

ABOUT THE AUTHOR

Judith C. Owens-Lalude

is the great-granddaughter of George Henry "Pap" Johnson, who was born in 1850 and was enslaved with his mother, Clarissa. They lived on Ben Miller's 600-acre farm in North Central Kentucky, now less than an hour's drive from Louisville, Kentucky, where Owens-Lalude grew up. After listening to tales told by her family's closest members about their ancestors, she wanted to know more. She visited the farm where her ancestors had been enslaved. She photographed outbuildings that were a part of her great-grandpa's and his mother's daily world.

Inspired to write a book, Owens-Lalude traveled to her husband's native Nigeria. She wanted to know the impact of enslavement on other Africans and African Americans for a better understanding of the history of slavery in the Americas; especially in Nelson and Spencer Counties, Kentucky, where her family lived. She was also intrigued by the writings of Harry Smith and Henry Johnson, who were two enslaved men who lived in the same regions as Owens-Lalude's family. From these readings, research, recordings, travels, and a powerful imagination, Owens-Lalude has written *The Long Walk: Slavery to Freedom,* a compelling novel.

National Park Service, National Underground Railroad Network to Freedom program has applied rigorous scholarship in identifying and awarding membership to more than 400 sites, programs and facilities in thirty-one states and the District of Columbia. Additional members are added twice a year. The first person interpretive program *Lucy Higgs Nichols,* by Judith C. Owens-Lalude, was accepted into the Network to Freedom as an interpretive program for students and adults

NATIONAL
UNDERGROUND RAILROAD
NETWORK TO FREEDOM